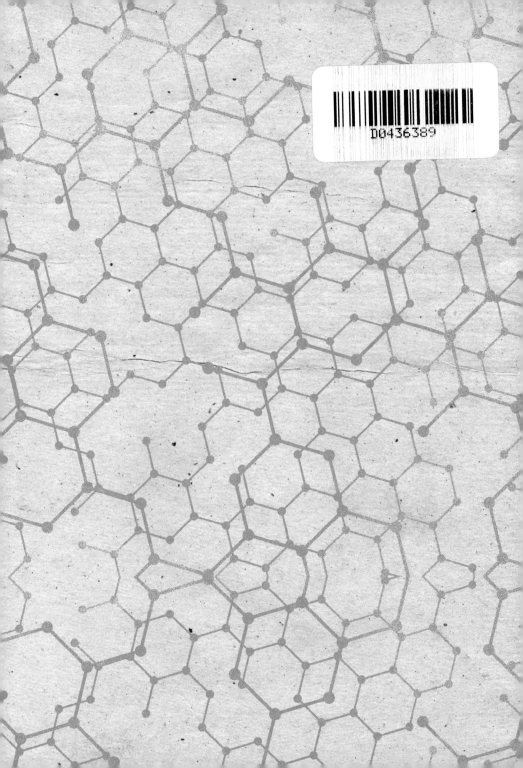

The ACADIA FILES

Book Three, Winter Science

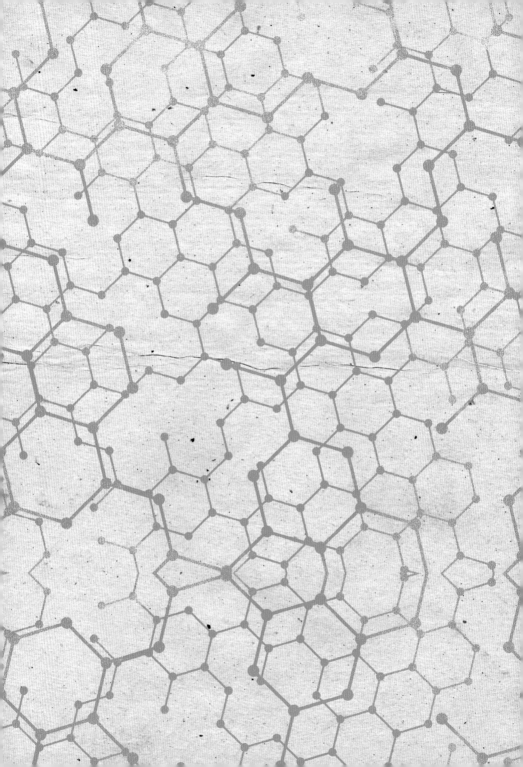

The ACADIA FILES

Book Three, Winter Science

Katie Coppens

Illustrated and designed by
Holly Hatam

TILBURY HOUSE PUBLISHERS, THOMASTON, MAINE

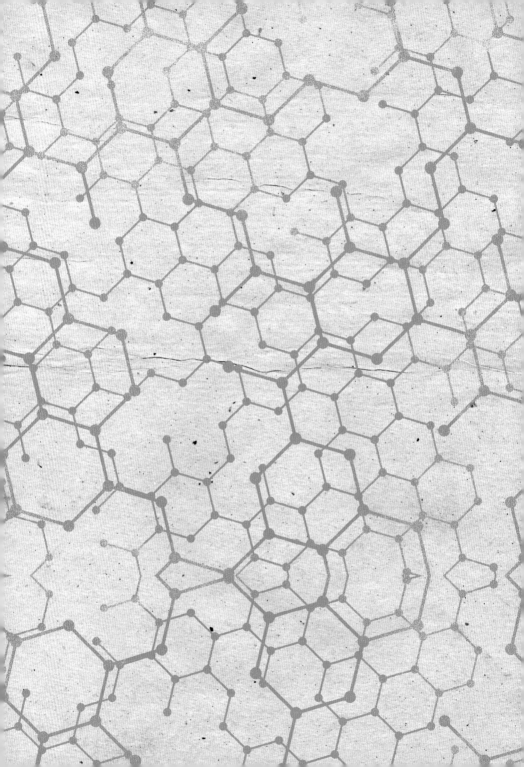

Contents

"Millions saw the apple fall,
but Newton asked why."

— Bernard Baruch

1
The Melting Snowman

Acadia and Isabel were on the same soccer team this fall, so they started having Friday night sleepovers before Saturday morning games. Soccer season is over now, but the weekly sleepovers continue. Why end a tradition that's so much fun? Waking up early one Saturday morning, the girls are delighted to see that the first snowfall of the winter has blanketed the yard during the night.

Isabel and Acadia play outside for hours, then decide to build a snowman. Unfortunately, the temperature has warmed up by late morning, and the sun is quickly melting the snow. The snowman they had hoped to build as tall as Acadia's dad turns out to be shorter than Acadia's dog, Baxter.

Acadia hands a scarf to Isabel. "You can put the final touch on the snowman—or should we call him a snow-toddler?"

When they stand back to admire their snow-toddler, Acadia notices a puddle at the foot of their creation. "Oh no, he's melting!"

"I don't get it," Isabel complains. "How can it snow one minute, then be sunny and warm the next?"

"Must be global warming. Wait. What *is* global warming?" Acadia asks.

"I don't know. Something about Earth warming? Poor little snow-dude, he deserved better."

"Acadia, Isabel, lunch!" yells Acadia's mom from the porch door.

"My parents said they were going to make pizza," Acadia tells Isabel. "They always use toppings to decorate it in some fun way. Want to eat, then come back out and see how our little snow-dude is doing?"

"Sounds good."

Acadia and Isabel run inside and look eagerly at the pizza. It's decorated like Earth; the oceans are white with cheese, and the continents are shaped with spinach.

"What do you think?" Acadia's dad asks.

"Is it a pun about global warming?" Acadia asks. "That would be so funny, because we were just talking about it."

"You mean, my daughter would finally have found one of my puns funny? But alas, no, it's supposed to be a pun about Earth's crust instead. Get it? Crust?"

"Oh, I get it. That's funny, Mr. Greene," Isabel says politely, while Acadia rolls her eyes.

"Why were you two talking about global warming?" Acadia's mom asks.

"We think that's why our snowman is melting. It snowed last night, but now it's sunny and warm," Acadia says.

"Is that what global warming is?" Isabel asks, as she and Acadia take off their coats.

"Not quite," Acadia's mom answers. "And it's usually called climate change rather than global warming now, because that's more accurate. Unlike 'weather,' which changes daily or even hourly, 'climate' is the average of weather patterns over a long period of time. When people say that the climate is changing, they mean Earth is showing long-term changes in its weather, including the amount of precipitation and the average temperature in a particular place."

"Does it really matter if the temperature changes a little?" Acadia asks.

Acadia's mom nods. "It sure does. A little temperature change, even a degree or two of warming, can make a big difference. You saw that today, when the temperature went up and caused your snowman to melt. The same thing is happening to the Arctic and Antarctic ice caps."

"What happens if the ice caps start to melt?" Isabel asks.

"When the ice melts into the ocean, it causes ocean levels to rise."

Acadia's dad pinches his index finger and thumb together. "And even a little bit of ocean rise could change coastlines around the world. Low-lying islands and some coastal cities might be flooded. It's already starting to happen."

As they all sit down at the table, Acadia's mom says, "And if the ocean temperature increases in some places, some of the plants and animals that live there may not be able to survive. That can have a big impact on the ocean's food chains. A few degrees can also impact how much rain we get. Some regions would get wetter, and others would get drier. There can be more wildfires. Hurricanes can get stronger because they're powered by heat from warm tropical oceans. We could have more flooding in some places and more droughts in others, which can impact farming and what food we can eat."

"You're scaring me!" Isabel says. "How did all this happen?"

"Scientists have looked at all the historical data they could find. They've noticed that since people have been creating more air pollution from things like factories and cars, Earth's average temperatures have been increasing," Acadia mom answers.

"Why?" Isabel asks.

"It's called the greenhouse effect. Do you know how a greenhouse works?"

Isabel nods. "We have a small one at school. The windows let in extra sunlight and heat, which gets trapped in there, so the plants grow really well."

"Yes," says Acadia's mom. "The problem is that too much carbon dioxide in the atmosphere does the same thing to our planet. The atmosphere surrounding our planet naturally traps heat, and that's good up to a point. But the carbon dioxide and other gases that are released when we burn fossil fuels result in too much heat being trapped."

"I've heard of having a carbon footprint. Does that have something to do with the greenhouse effect?" Isabel asks.

"Yes it does! Your carbon footprint is how much you contribute to the greenhouse effect. Think about how you get to school, for example. Someone who rides her bike or walks has a smaller carbon footprint than someone who gets dropped off in a car."

Acadia asks, "Is there anything we can do to reduce our carbon footprint?"

"We can make sure we take the bus to school instead of getting dropped off," Isabel offers. "One bus carrying forty kids probably has a smaller carbon footprint than forty cars each carrying one kid."

"Absolutely!" says Acadia's mom. "And fuel isn't just used for cars. It's also used to make the stuff we own."

"I never really thought about it before, but a used soccer ball is better for the environment than a brand-new one, and it works just as well," Acadia says.

Isabel adds, "Maybe we could start a club at school to teach other kids about their carbon footprints."

Acadia looks at the fruit bowl and notices a kiwi with a "Grown in New Zealand" sticker on it. "Even something simple, like eating a kiwi, has an impact," she says. "That kiwi traveled across half the planet, from New Zealand to Maine. That's a lot of gas for boats and trucks!"

"Maybe we could ask the school's cafeteria to buy apples from Maine instead of fruit from far away," Isabel suggests.

"You two are right. Buying items that are grown or made nearby is a great start, and it helps local businesses. We can also plant trees, which help absorb some pollutants. And we can . . . ."

Acadia points at the pizza, saying, "We can be sure not to waste delicious food, because it took energy to get the ingredients from the farms to the grocery store and then to us!"

"Not to mention the energy needed to heat it in the oven," says Acadia's dad as he hands out slices to everyone.

Acadia takes a big bite and smiles. "Yum! At least *this* Earth is the perfect temperature."

Later that day, Acadia makes a list of the foods in her kitchen. She examines the labels on each item to see where it came from, and then she researches how far that food traveled from where it was grown or produced to get to her house in Maine. She sees her mom's grocery list on the refrigerator and adds some suggested substitutions of local foods.

Then she looks for other ways to reduce her carbon footprint. Some things surprise her. She hadn't realized that flushing the toilet uses energy to get the water to her house and then to transport and treat the waste-water. And shower water has to be heated as well as transported and treated. Acadia learns that each of the following activities adds 2.2 pounds (1 kg) of CO_2 to her personal carbon footprint:

* making a journey of 7 miles (12 km) by public transportation (train or bus);

* riding 3.75 miles (6 km) in a fuel-efficient car;

* flying 1.4 miles (2.2 km) in a plane;

* operating a computer for 32 hours;

* throwing away five plastic bags;

* throwing away two plastic bottles;

* eating a third of a cheeseburger.

By the time she finishes, Acadia has a lot of ideas in mind to reduce her impact on Earth.

Food Miles

Food in my house	Where it's from	Approximate distance traveled to my house
Kiwi	New Zealand	9,320 miles (15,000 Km)
Box of Mac n' Cheese	Berkeley, California	3,200 miles (5,150 Km)
Clementine	Delano, California	3,150 miles (5,070 Km)
Tea	England	3,100 miles (4,990 Km)
Coffee	Colombia	2,725 miles (4,385 Km)
Banana	Honduras	2,300 miles (3,700 Km)
Tortilla Chips	Irving, Texas	1,900 miles (3,060 Km)
Orange Juice	Bradenton, Florida	1,500 miles (2,415 Km)
Cereal	Minneapolis, Minnesota	1,500 miles (2,415 Km)
Cheese Sticks	Green Bay, Wisconsin	1,300 miles (2,090 Km)
Hot Cocoa	Chicago, Illinois	1,100 miles (1,770 Km)
Salsa	Westport, Connecticut	275 miles (440 Km)
Maple Syrup	Websterville, Vermont	240 miles (386 Km)
Potato Chips (Dad's favorite)	Hyannis, MA	195 miles (315 Km)
Apple	Turner, Maine	30 miles (48 Km)
Milk	Portland, Maine	18 miles (29 Km)

Breakfast Club

Reducing Our Carbon Footprint by Going Greene! (Dad will love this pun!)

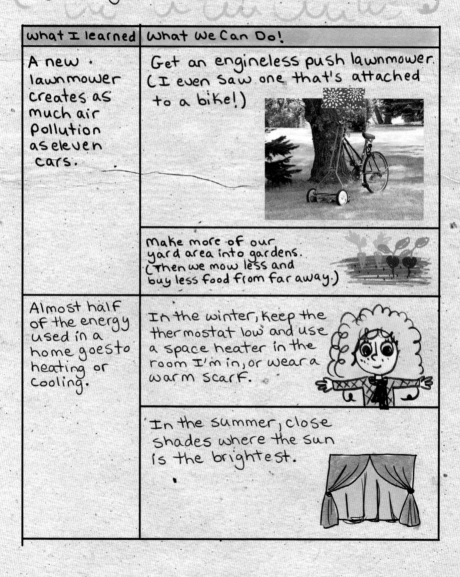

what I learned	What We Can Do!
A new lawnmower creates as much air pollution as eleven cars.	Get an engineless push lawnmower. (I even saw one that's attached to a bike!)
	Make more of our yard area into gardens. (Then we mow less and buy less food from far away.)
Almost half of the energy used in a home goes to heating or cooling.	In the winter, keep the thermostat low and use a space heater in the room I'm in, or wear a warm scarf.
	In the summer, close shades where the sun is the brightest.

Lights use energy when we're not in the room, and electronics can use energy even when they're not being used. Much of the electricity carried through powerlines is generated by burning fossil fuels.	Turn off lights when I leave a room. Unplug "vampire" electronics like smartphone chargers and game consoles, which consume energy even when they're not being used.
About 3 to 4% of energy consumption is used to move, clean, and dispose of household water and wastewater—and that doesn't include the energy used to heat the water for my showers. The average person uses 88 gallons of water per day.	Use a watering can to capture shower water while I wait for the water to warm up. Install a low-flow shower head. Don't let the water run when I'm brushing my teeth or washing dishes. Start the dishwasher and washing machine only when we have a full load. Drain rainwater from the gutters into a rain barrel, and use this water for the garden.

It takes a million years for a glass bottle to break down in a land fill.	Instead of buying drinks that come in a bottle, make my own drinks.
	Recycle and compost everything I can. Set a family goal of only one trash bag per week.
We use about 1 1/2 plastic straws per person each day, on average.	Ask my school to stop handing out straws with milk cartons.
	Ask for no straw with any drink we get at a restaurant.
Around 13% of all landfill waste is plastic.	Use tap water in a reusable bottle instead of buying plastic bottles.
	Try to have my school lunch create no trash by using reusable containers.

NEW SCIENCE WORDS

Atmosphere

The gases that surround our planet. Some layers of our atmosphere are:

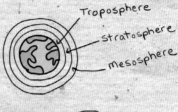

Troposphere
Stratosphere
Mesosphere

Carbon Footprint

How much of an impact we cause from the fossil fuels we burn. Riding in a car, taking a shower, mowing the lawn, turning on lights, watching TV, cooking a meal, and heating our houses are some of the activities that use power and produce greenhouse gases.

Fossil fuels are used to make the car and for the gasoline to drive it... a bigger car uses even more!

Fossil fuels are used to make the bike. Your energy powers it!

Climate

The long-term average conditions produced by local or global weather patterns.

Climate Change

The name we give to the long-term environmental changes caused by burning fossil fuels, which adds carbon dioxide and other greenhouse gases to Earth's atmosphere. Climate changes include global warming; sea-level rise; ice loss in Greenland, Antarctica, the Arctic, and mountain glaciers; shifts in the times of plant blooming; and extreme weather events.

NEW SCIENCE WORDS

Fossil Fuels

Fuels like oil, coal, and natural gas that are formed over millions of years by dead organisms decomposing underground. Fossil fuels release carbon dioxide to the atmosphere when they're burned. Burning a gallon of gas in our family car produces 19 pounds of CO_2.

Fuel type	CO_2 emitted
Gasoline	19 pounds/gallon (2.3 Kg/liter)
Diesel	22 pounds/gallon (2.7 Kg/liter)
Heating oil	25 pounds/gallon (3.0 Kg/liter)

Global Warming

The upward trend in worldwide average temperatures due to the increase in fossil fuel emissions since the industrial revolution.

I'm so HOT!

Greenhouse Effect

Carbon dioxide, methane, and other gases act like the glass roof of a greenhouse, trapping heat in the atmosphere so it doesn't radiate as quickly into space. This causes Earth to get warmer over time.

Sun

outgoing energy

Incoming energy

Atmosphere, containing greenhouse gases

Trapped energy

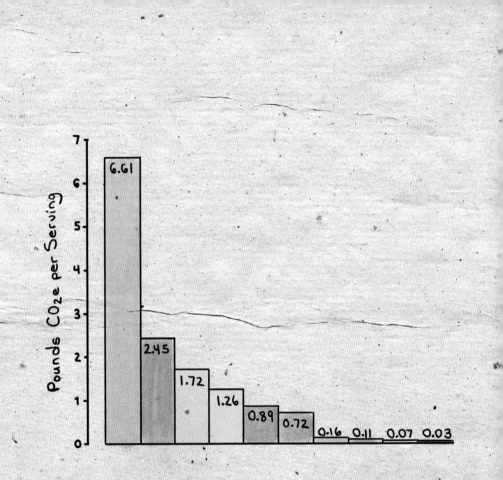

Pounds CO₂e per Serving

- 6.61
- 2.45
- 1.72
- 1.26
- 0.89
- 0.72
- 0.16
- 0.11
- 0.07
- 0.03

Beef
Cheese
Pork
Poultry
Eggs

Milk
Rice
Legumes
Carrots
Potatoes

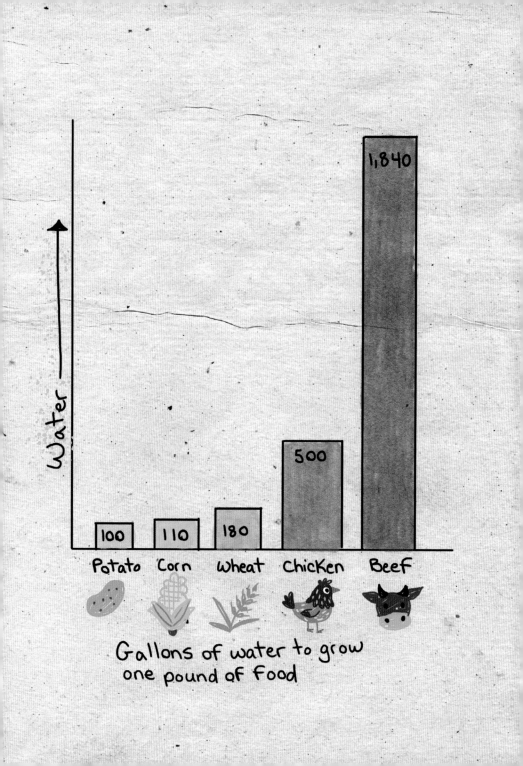

Water

1,840

500

100 110 180

Potato Corn Wheat Chicken Beef

Gallons of water to grow
one pound of food

Things I Still Wonder:

- A long time ago, when there weren't highways or supermarkets, how did people get food? What food did they eat in the winter?

- How much less will my carbon footprint be if I eat food that is grown locally?

- What are some other things I can do to reduce my carbon footprint?

2
Why Balloons Float

As the final guests attending Acadia's eleventh birthday party head out the door, Acadia waves goodbye and walks back into the kitchen.

"That was a fun party," Acadia's dad says as he scoops up wrapping paper from the floor.

Acadia gets down on her hands and knees to retrieve some wrapping paper from under the table. "I liked the cake decorated like a soccer ball," she says. "That was pretty cool."

"Well, 'pretty cool' is what we go for around here," her dad says. "So do you feel older and wiser? Eleven's a good age, isn't it?"

"I guess, but I thought I'd feel . . . I don't know, I guess I just feel the same."

"How'd you think you'd feel?"

"Smarter, maybe."

"You're pretty smart, kiddo."

"Sometimes I think I am." Acadia sits down in a chair with a helium balloon tied to its back. "Like, I get why you should never, ever release a helium balloon outside. Balloons are really bad for animals."

"And power lines! You've learned a lot about the environment this year," Acadia's dad says.

Acadia pulls the balloon down and watches it float back up. "But there's still a lot I don't know. Like, why does this balloon float?"

"Do you really want to know?"

Just then Acadia's mom walks into the kitchen. "That was a fun party!" she says. "It was so nice of you to invite Joshua."

"Hold on, Mom. I'm getting smarter."

"Maybe you can answer your own question," Acadia's dad says. "What do we call this kind of balloon?"

"It's a helium balloon."

"And why do we call it that?"

"Because it's filled with helium. That's what's in the tank they fill it with, right?"

"Yes. So, how are helium balloons different from regular balloons?"

"That's easy. When we blow up a regular balloon, it's filled with the air we breathe out. But I still don't get what makes helium balloons float."

"Well, did you know that helium is lighter than air?"

"Hold on! How can something be lighter than air? Air doesn't weigh anything."

"Ah, but it does. All matter has mass . . . ."

Acadia furrows her eyebrows.

"Everything has atoms in it," her dad continues, "so everything takes up space and therefore weighs something. Each type of atom has a different weight. The weight of each atom matters because . . . ."

"I'm eleven now, Dad—not thirty. Please keep it in kid words. What is an adam?"

"Not an adam, an *atom*. An atom is very, very, very small—so small that you could never see one with your naked eye or even with a regular microscope. *Everything* is made up of atoms."

"Are they like cells?"

"Much, much smaller. All living things have cells, but *all things* have atoms: living things, dead things, and things that have never been alive—rocks, metals, gases, you name it. This table is made of atoms. Water is made of atoms. *You* are made of atoms."

"So are cells made of atoms?"

"Yes. *Everything* is made of atoms."

"Okay. So what does an atom's weight have to do with helium being lighter than air?"

"Well, air is made up mostly of nitrogen and oxygen."

"I thought air was just *air.*"

"Not quite! Everything, including air, is made of elements."

"Slow down for a second. So everything is made of elements *and* atoms?"

"Elements are just names for different types of atoms. Each element has an atomic weight, which is how much one atom of the element weighs. One atom of the element called helium is very light."

"But air must be light too, because it's, well, air."

"Air is a mixture of nitrogen and oxygen, and you're right—those elements are also very light. But helium atoms weigh even less than nitrogen and oxygen atoms."

"Is helium the lightest element?"

"It's the second lightest of all the elements. Hydrogen is the lightest."

"Where's hydrogen?"

"Pretty much everywhere. Have you ever heard of H_2O?"

"Yes. That's a fancy way of saying water."

"Yes, and it's called H_2O because a water molecule is two hydrogen atoms bonded with a single oxygen atom. When atoms bond, they make a molecule. The symbol for hydrogen is H, and the symbol for oxygen is O. Two H's and one O make a water molecule."

"There's just so much to learn. Okay, let me think about all this in a way that makes sense to me. Let's pretend this black frosting is one element—we'll call it chocolatium—and the white frosting is another element, vanillium. One atom of chocolatium weighs more than one atom of vanillium. It has a higher atomic weight.

And if I squish an atom of each frosting element together I get a molecule."

"Yes, and that sounds delicious." Acadia's dad swipes some black and white frosting off the cake, then squishes them together and eats them.

Acadia pulls down the balloon, then watches it rise up again and thinks about different things that can float. "I'm starting to get it . . . . But how does a boat float? Some boats are made of metal, and metal atoms must be way heavier than water. You said water is made of hydrogen and oxygen."

"The answer to that question is the key to why balloons float, too. Wait here—I'll be right back."

Acadia's dad heads downstairs to the basement, and Acadia and her mom hear him clattering around down there. Acadia rolls her eyes, and her mom smiles as if she knows what her husband is up to. He comes back up the stairs with a bucket and an empty glass bottle that's sealed with a cork stopper. He fills the bucket with water from the kitchen faucet and sets it on the floor. Then he puts the bottle in the bucket and steps back triumphantly. "Ta da!" he exclaims.

Acadia is underwhelmed. "It's floating," she says. "Why is that a big deal?"

"Because the glass bottle's atoms are heavier than water's atoms, but the bottle floats anyway," her dad says. "The secret is the air inside the bottle. Air is *much* lighter than water. So the bottle sinks until it displaces a volume of water that weighs as much as the bottle. Once it reaches that point, it floats. And, as you can see, a big part of the bottle is still above water."

Acadia furrows her brow again. "Dad, you keep forgetting that I'm only eleven. What does 'displaces' mean?"

"Maybe I can help," says Acadia's mom. "It means taking the place of something else. The bottle is able to float because it displaces some of the water."

"So if we add water to the bottle, making it heavier, will the bottle need to displace more water to be able to float?" Acadia asks.

"Good thinking! Let's try it and find out," Acadia's dad says.

When they add a little water, the bottle still floats, but it is deeper in the bucket because it's displacing more water. When Acadia fills the bottle halfway, it displaces even more water, floating with only its neck above water.

Then Acadia fills the bottle completely with water and corks it. "I think we can all guess what will happen to the bottle now," she says with a smile as she places it in the bucket. Sure enough, it sinks instantly, making an audible tapping sound when it hits the bottom of the bucket.

"So let's get back to the balloon," Acadia's dad says, pulling the balloon down from the ceiling, then letting it float back up. "The balloon is made of metal foil, which is heavier than air, but it's full of helium, which is lighter—less dense—than air, so why does the balloon float?"

Acadia thinks about what she saw with the bottle. "The balloon is—I'm going to try to be fancy here— *displacing* a volume of air that weighs more than it does, so the balloon floats."

Acadia parents smile and start to say something, but Acadia continues, "Hold on, I'm not done yet . . . ." She tugs on the balloon and pictures how it will change over the next few days. It will slowly lose helium and eventually sink to the ground. "That's why helium balloons sink when they deflate," she says. "The balloon stops floating when it becomes heavier than the air it displaces."

Acadia's dad says, "Very impressive! I think eleven's going to be a good year for you."

Acadia looks up at the colorful balloon. "I think so too."

Acadia decides to use the balloon for an investigation. She wants to see if she can add weight to the balloon and get it to float between the ceiling and the floor, where it neither sinks or rises. Acadia's dad says this is called *neutral buoyancy*.

My Neutral Buoyancy Experiment

My Question: Can I get a balloon to float at neutral buoyancy?

Research: Neutral buoyancy is achieved when the weight of the thing doing the displacing is exactly equal to the weight of the stuff displaced by that thing.

My experimental method:

I first used the balloon's ribbon to attach a paper cup, but it was too heavy. I trimmed down the cup, but then it was too light. So I tried adding different materials to the cup and realized that cotton balls work best because they are light and can easily be made smaller. Dad said it looked like a hot-air balloon, and he drew a little dude that I put in the cup. At neutral buoyancy, the balloon was at my eye level and looked very cool floating around the house!

NEW SCIENCE WORDS

Element

Something that is so pure that it cannot be broken down into other things. Some elements I have heard of:

Hydrogen
Symbol = H
Atomic Weight = 1

Helium
Symbol = He
Atomic Weight = 4

Oxygen
Symbol = O
Atomic Weight = 16

Gold
Symbol = Au
Atomic Weight = 197

Lead
Symbol = Pb
Atomic Weight = 207.

Atom

One very small part of an element.

one gold ring has over...
60,000,000,000,000,000,000,000,000
ATOMS!

Molecule

When atoms bond together.

One water molecule = H_2O

2 Hydrogen + 1 Oxygen
atoms   atom

A very zoomed-in picture of the molecule:

Things I Still Wonder:

- How is a giant cruise ship able to float on water? (My dad told me to learn about Archimedes' principle. He said something about an ancient Greek guy doing science while taking a bath. Is that multitasking?)

- Are the elements on other planets the same as on Earth?

- How does the periodic table of elements work?

Before going to sleep, Acadia opens her curtains so she can watch the snow falling in the night. The snow looks heavy and fast against the halo of the streetlight. She hopes it will keep falling that way through the night, and it does! In the morning, she's delighted to learn that school has been called off, and she's even more excited when she finds out that Isabel and Joshua will be spending the day with her.

After playing in the snow for hours—building forts and throwing snowballs—the kids head inside for a well-deserved lunch.

"What do you want to do after we eat?" Acadia asks the group. "Should we go back outside or watch a movie?"

Acadia's dad puts a plate of grilled cheese sandwiches in front of them. "I was thinking we could have a paper airplane contest," he says, hopefully.

"That sounds like fun!" Joshua says.

"Sure!" says Isabel.

Mr. Greene dashes off, and just as the kids are polishing off the sandwich platter, he returns with an armload of paper in assorted sizes and thicknesses. "Do you want to just make them, or do you want me to give you some tips?" he asks. It's obvious to all three kids that he's itching to give them tips.

"I'd like some tips, please," Isabel answers. "I don't know anything about paper airplanes, except that mine never seem to fly."

"First, show me how you make one," Acadia's dad says.

Each child folds an airplane and does a test throw. None of them go far—especially Isabel's, which plummets to the ground about a foot in front of her.

"See? I really don't know anything about paper airplanes," Isabel says.

"Okay, first off, the most important thing you need to know about making a paper airplane is that it requires a good *altitude*," Acadia's dad says, smiling at the group.

"You see what I did there? I said altitude instead of atti-tude. Altitude is an object's height above the ground."

Acadia shakes her head. "Dad, most people don't speak in puns."

"Okay, okay, you clearly don't understand the *gravity* of this situation," Acadia's dad adds, snickering at his own humor.

"Dad," Acadia whispers, "you're embarrassing me."

"Okay, I'll be serious. Let's talk about what it means to be aerodynamic."

"Is that another pun?" Joshua asks.

Acadia's dad grins and shakes his head. "Nope. Being aerodynamic is what helps a plane stay in the air. The design of the airplane helps fight gravity. Isabel, I remem-ber how well you understood gravity. Please remind everyone what gravity is."

"Uh, you saw how my plane fell really fast? That was gravity." Isabel smiles. "It's a force that pulls things toward Earth."

"That's right," says Acadia's dad. "So you need to fight gravity. And you can do that by giving the plane well-designed wings, which create lift." He quickly folds a paper airplane with large wings extending outward from its body, or fuselage. "Gravity is pulling the plane down, so you want to give your plane all the lift you can."

"So bigger wings are good?" Isabel asks.

"Up to a point. If the wings are *too* big, all that surface area will create too much drag, and drag is what slows your plane down."

All three kids look confused. "Explain drag, please," says Acadia.

"Gladly!" says Acadia's dad. "Drag is caused by the resistance of air to anything traveling through it. Air is made of molecules, and any object moving through air has to continually push those molecules out of the way. Doing that causes drag, and the bigger the object, the more drag it has to overcome in order to keep moving."

"Um, Dad, school was called off today," Acadia mumbles.

"Don't be a *drag,* Acadia," Joshua says, smiling at Acadia's dad. "Get it, *drag?*"

"Good one, Joshua." Acadia's dad gives him a high five. Then he says, "Think about how much harder it is to walk into a strong wind than to walk in still air. Have you ever thought about why that is? It's because the wind is really trillions and trillions of air molecules pushing against you. Now imagine that you can run very, very fast. The only problem is, the faster you run, even in still air, the more resistance you'll encounter from the air you're pushing aside, and at some point that drag will get so big that you can't go any faster."

"Wait, so if we can't make our wings too big, how do we get lift?" Isabel asks. "Can we set up a fan to help keep our planes in the air?"

"Nope, that would be cheating. Lift comes from good design. Bigger wings provide more lift but also create more drag. A good design will provide more lift and less drag, which is easy to say but hard to do. That's where the science of aerodynamics comes in. An aerodynamic design is all about getting the most lift and speed with the least drag and thrust."

"Stop right there, Dad," says Acadia. "What's thrust?"

"Thrust is the power that makes the plane go. A real plane gets thrust from its engines, but yours gets thrust from the way you throw it."

"That's the fun part," Joshua says.

"And the other fun part is building it. These sheets of paper have different weights and sizes. Think about drag and lift when you try out your designs."

"Can we start now?" Joshua asks, reaching for a sheet of the lightest paper he can see.

"Hold on. Sorry, Acadia, I have to say it . . . . 'May the *force* be with you.'"

Ignoring the nonstop puns, Acadia, Isabel, and Joshua start folding paper and testing airplanes. The middle of the table fills with rejected planes, but with each failed design they learn from their mistakes. When it is time to compete, the three airplanes look totally different. Joshua's is small and lightweight, Acadia's has giant wings, and Isabel's has a long, pointed tip.

"Okay, this is the starting line," Acadia's dad says, laying a yardstick on the floor. "Before you throw your plane, explain what you were thinking when you made the design."

"I'll go," Joshua says. "I made mine as light as I could, hoping that would improve lift." Joshua pulls his arm back and quickly throws the airplane, which travels about half the length of the kitchen. Everyone claps.

"Good thinking. Who's next? Isabel?"

"Okay. I wanted it to be aero—what's that word?"

"Aerodynamic."

"Yes, I wanted it to be aerodynamic, so I made it really pointy, thinking that would help it cut through the air. And I used paper that was light, but not too light, thinking that would help too."

"Why didn't you want to use paper that was too light?" Acadia's dad asks.

"I tested it with tissue paper and it didn't dart through the air the way I wanted it to. Really heavy paper had too much drag, I think. This medium-weight paper seemed to work best." Isabel looks a little nervous as she pulls her arm back and throws the airplane, but it travels so fast and straight that it hits the far kitchen wall. Everyone cheers for Isabel as she runs over to pick it up.

"Great job! Last but not least is my darling daughter, Acadia."

"I decided to go more for style. My plane does something cool when I throw it. I think the big wings make it catch too much air, so it actually spins." Acadia throws the plane up high toward the ceiling. On its way back down, it quickly spins and twirls so fast that no one can tell where one wing ends and the other begins.

"It didn't go far, but it sure looked neat," Acadia's dad says.

"Do it again, Acadia. That was so cool!" Joshua says.

Acadia picks the plane up and throws it toward the ceiling even harder, causing it to spin even faster. "Can we make another one?" Acadia asks.

"Absolutely. How about if each of you tries another *approach*?" Acadia's dad answers. "Get it, *approach*?"

Acadia rolls her eyes, then smiles at her dad. "You know what they say: Time flies when you're having *pun*."

After more explorations, Acadia's dad makes one more plane for the group, explaining that this design holds the world record for paper airplane flight distance: 226 feet, 10 inches. Each of them tries throwing it, but it travels so far that they need to take it outside for an accurate test. They don't get close to the world record, but the flights are impressive. Acadia writes down the steps to build this plane and draws some step-by-step sketches in her science notebook. She also adds sketches of the airplanes she and her friends came up with. She's proud of her own original design.

How to build the world's best
paper airplane

1. Hold the paper the long way. Fold the top right corner down to the left edge.

2. Make a sharp crease, then unfold.

3. Repeat with the top left corner of the paper, folding it down to the right edge.

4. Make a sharp crease, then unfold.

5. Fold the top right corner until it touches the crease you made in step 2.

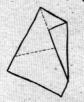

6. Make another sharp crease, then unfold.

7. Fold the top left corner until it touches the crease you made in Step 4.

8. Make a sharp crease, and this time do not unfold.

9. Return the right corner to the crease you made in Step 6, and this time do not unfold. (This fold will overlap slightly with the fold you made in Step 8.)

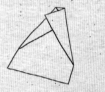

10. Lay the folded paper flat with the pointy end facing away from you. We'll label that end "A", and we'll label the place where the two folds cross each other "B".

11. Fold "A" toward you to make a sharp side-to-side crease in the paper at "B". Do not unfold.

12. Fold what is now the top right corner down over the edge of the fold you created in Step 9. Make a sharp crease along fold C, and do not unfold.

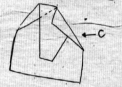

13. Repeat Step 12 with the top left corner, making a sharp crease along the fold you created in Step 8, fold D.

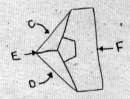

14. Turn the paper over, and fold in half between points "E" and "F," folding the paper's two long edges upward so they come together. These will be the plane's wings.

15. Put a finger on the plane's tip at point "E" to anchor it, and fold the top wing down so that the wing's trailing edge touches point F. Make a sharp crease there.

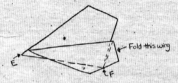

16. Repeat with the other wing so the wings are the same size. Make another sharp crease.

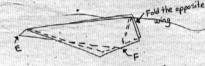

17. Grasp the airplane near its tip and...

18. Let it FLY! Adjust the wing angles between flights until they're ideal.

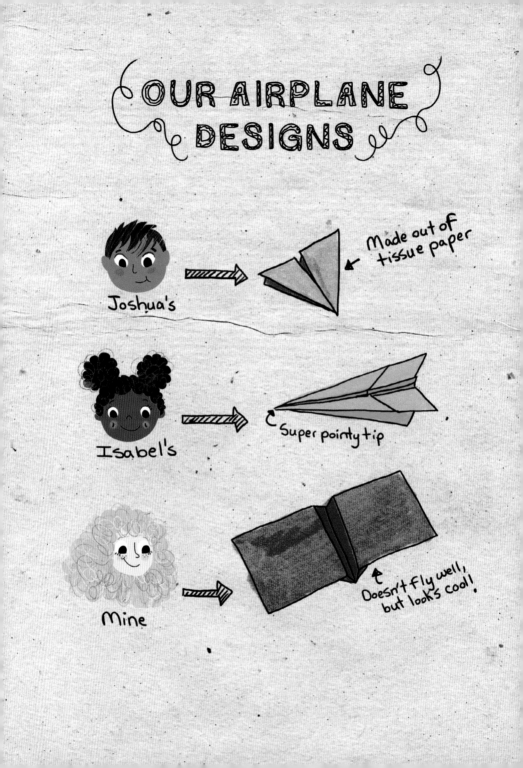

NEW SCIENCE WORDS

Aerodynamic

Having a good shape to move through air. A good airplane design reduces drag and increases lift.

Drag

The resistance to an object's movement through a fluid like air or water. Drag is caused by the friction of the fluid's molecules against the object's surface. The more surface area the object has, the more drag it creates. Water creates more drag than air because it's a denser fluid.

Lift

The force that enables a heavier-than-air object to stay up in the air.

Thrust

The force that propels (or pushes) an object forward.

Lift
Drag
Thrust
Gravity

Things I Still Wonder:

- What happens if I make "the world's best paper airplane" from different types of paper? What type of paper works the best?

- How is an actual airplane able to stay in the air? Does this connect at all to understanding how a boat can float on water?

Acadia steps off the school bus and walks up her icy driveway. As the cold wind hits her face, she quickly pulls her backpack around and looks in the front zipper for her house key, but notices it's not there.

"Please tell me I didn't forget it," she mumbles to herself as she frantically searches her coat pockets.

Acadia zips her winter coat all the way up and tries to warm up her hands by blowing on them, but all she sees is the miniature clouds created by her frozen breath. She realizes she will have to find another way to get warm. She could walk to Joshua's house, which would be the simplest option, but Acadia decides to problem-solve a different way.

"Animals survive outside all winter. I can make it twenty minutes until Mom gets home," Acadia mutters, plunking herself down on the front steps.

Huddled on the stairs, she looks up at the bare maple tree without a single leaf. She looks over at the icy white snow in her front yard that seems hard enough to ice skate on. She looks at the paw tracks from Baxter's footprints in the driveway and the boot marks from where her family has walked. She listens to the fierce howling of the wind and notices that she hears nothing else, not even a bird. She looks around at the empty yard and wonders where all the animals have gone.

Acadia knows some birds fly south to warmer places or to places that have more food, but where do all the other animals go? Where do the frogs go that live in the pond? Where do the squirrels and chipmunks go that drive Baxter crazy when they run around the yard in the spring, summer, and fall? Where do the bees go that she sees flying from flower to flower on hot summer days? She looks down at her puffy coat, which is the only thing protecting her from the weather. If she's this cold, how are all those other animals surviving?

Acadia walks toward the maple tree to see if she can find any signs of life, but there is nothing at all on the tree, just an empty nest resting among its bare branches. She listens for animals but hears only Baxter's faint barking as he watches her from the kitchen window. Then, as she heads back to the house, she sees her mom's car pull into the driveway.

"Mom, you're home early."

"You forgot this." Acadia's mom holds up a key. "I rushed home. I was worried that you'd be waiting outside in the cold, which I now see is exactly what you are doing." She puts her arm around her daughter's shoulders. "Why didn't you go to Joshua's house? Why did you wait outside?"

"Mom, where do all the animals go?"

"What do you mean?"

"It's really cold out. How do animals survive in the winter?"

Acadia's mom opens the door, and they head into the kitchen. "The animals all have different ways of surviving," Acadia's mom says. "Some animals leave for the winter and migrate to other places. That's what many birds and butterflies do."

"Isabel's grandparents do that too. They leave Maine in November to stay down in Florida during the winter, then come back in April when it starts to get warm."

"That's very smart of them."

"But how do the creatures that stay here survive?" Acadia asks as she takes off her coat and sits down at the kitchen table.

Acadia's mom sits down beside her. "Some animals hibernate," she says.

"I know bears hibernate, but how do other creatures survive?"

"Bears aren't the only ones that hibernate. Some bats hibernate too, and so do turtles, snakes, and frogs."

"Frogs? Tell me about frogs!" Acadia says, thinking about the letter she wrote to the town council in the fall about protecting the frogs at Rearis Pond. [See *The Acadia Files: Book Two, Autumn Science.*]

Acadia's mom smiles. "Frogs find a perfect spot—sheltered from predators and the worst of the weather—and go into a sleepy state until spring. Some, like bullfrogs, dig into the mud at the bottom of a pond. Others do what toads do: They dig deep burrows on land, in soft soil, getting down below the frost line. And others, like wood frogs and spring peepers, seek out cracks in rocks or logs or cover themselves with leaf litter. Then their body functions get really, really slow, so they burn very little energy and can live through the winter on their stored reserves of fat."

"What are body functions?"

"Like their breathing and blood flow."

"Do they freeze?"

"Not totally. Their skin and outer tissues might freeze, but their blood is like antifreeze, and it keeps their organs from freezing solid. A partially frozen frog might stop breathing, and its heart might stop beating, but when it thaws out it comes back to life!"

Acadia thinks about that for a minute. "Trees are kind of like frogs," she says. "Deciduous trees drop leaves, and everything kind of slows down so they can survive. It's kind of creepy that there are all these sleeping, half-frozen animals and trees out there."

"Some stay awake, like honey bees, but we don't see them over the winter. They stay in their hive and eat stored honey. There can be thousands of bees in the hive, and their energy from moving around helps keep the hive warm."

"It's neat that the winter is like a different world for animals. They have to act totally different to survive. The only difference for us is that we have to wear big coats."

"But our coats aren't enough. We need warm houses to survive. If you ever forget your key again, please go to Joshua's house."

"Okay, I will. I just wanted to see what it would feel like to have to survive. It was cold!"

"Not all creatures survive the winter. Have you ever heard the term 'natural selection?'"

"Yes, it has to do with adaptations. The plants or animals that are the best adapted to their environment are the most likely to live. Is that what happens in the winter? Those less adapted to survive are more likely to die?"

"Often, yes. For example, white-tailed deer store extra body fat under their skin to help them survive cold temperatures and the shortage of food in the winter. The most well-adapted animals are most able to find food in the summer and fall to build up their fat reserves. The deer that aren't as quick or as good at finding food don't build up enough stored fat."

"So deer can die of starvation?"

"There is a lot of competition for food among animals, and the strongest and fastest are usually the ones to live."

"That stinks for the weak ones," Acadia says, looking sad.

"It does, but that also means that only the best-adapted deer are reproducing. Remember when we talked about genetics? Strong, fast parents should make strong, fast baby deer."

"Is that why it's called natural selection? It's almost like nature selects what will most likely live or die. That really does stink for the weak ones."

"Humans are animals too, but we're pretty lucky compared to all the animals that live outside."

"We sure are. Not only do we have puffy coats and warm houses, but . . ." Acadia raises her eyebrow at her mom, "we also have hot chocolate."

"And we have marshmallows too," Acadia's mom says, reaching for two mugs and the bag of marshmallows. She tosses a soft, puffy marshmallow to Acadia.

Acadia catches it and plops it into her mouth. "Yep, it's way better in here than out there."

A few days later, after a fresh snowfall, Acadia and her mom go on a winter walk. They find tracks left by many types of creatures, and Acadia's mom teaches Acadia that tracks can tell a story. Acadia takes photographs of the tracks and uses them to make inferences.

Back home, Acadia adds the photos to her science notebook, along with some notes about each type of track.

Animal Tracks

These must be deer tracks, because deer have cloven hooves. I think a deer stopped in its path and stood here for a while. The yellowish color in the snow makes me think the deer peed while it was standing here.

I think these tracks might be a bunny going from left to right. The hind feet are bigger than the forepaws, and they land in front of the forepaws when the rabbit is hopping.

The big tracks on the left are from a wild turkey, and the smaller tracks are from some kind of mammal, maybe a squirrel or raccoon. My guess is that these animals were walking at different times. I wonder why they both chose to walk here?

This was our best find! My mom was so excited! She said a bird of prey (maybe an owl) swooped down and caught something - maybe a field mouse or a chipmunk! You can see the wing and talon marks in the snow!

Here are more animal tracks. They are from Mom and me!

Mom's boots

My boots

How Animals Survive in the Winter

The arctic hare's fur turns white in the winter to help it camouflage with the snow. This helps it avoid predators. In the spring, it turns grayish.

Chipmunks have cheeks that stretch so they can gather extra food in the fall. They stuff their cheeks full of seeds.

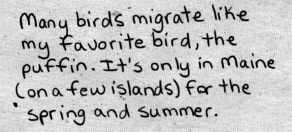

Many birds migrate like my favorite bird, the puffin. It's only in Maine (on a few islands) for the spring and summer.

NEW SCIENCE WORDS

Adaptation

Something that helps an organism survive.

can hear well

great night vision

sharp beak

Silent flight

strong talons

Hibernation

Slowing down an organism's body into a sleepy state.

Migration

Changing locations... Sometimes to the other side of the world!

Natural Selection

The organisms that are best adapted live, while others die.

The fastest live!

sorry!

Things I Still Wonder:

- When animals migrate, how do they know how to get where they're going for the winter, and how to return in the spring?

- Do animals often have babies in the spring so they are bigger, stronger, and more independent by the time winter comes, and more likely to survive the cold?

Acadia, Isabel and Joshua trudge through a fresh layer of snow, pulling their sleds behind them. Walking down her road, Acadia notices how the bright sunlight illuminates the powdery snow.

"I think this could be the last snow of the year," Acadia says.

Isabel looks down at the ground. "Yep, it'll be spring soon, and all of this will be gone."

"Then we'd better get in some good sledding today!" Joshua yells as he grabs the rope of his snow tube and starts to run up the hill.

"Slow down! It's not a race," Acadia calls after him.

He turns back. "Let's make it a race. Let's see which sled can go the farthest."

"Sounds fun," Isabel says, running to catch up with Joshua.

"Wait for me!" Acadia shouts.

At the top of the hill, the sunlight feels even stronger as it reflects off the bright, white snow. The wind is mild and refreshing, not bitterly cold like it was a few weeks before. The three stand atop the hill in descending order of height: Isabel, Acadia, and Joshua. Isabel is holding a plastic rectangular sled, Acadia a large round saucer sled, and Joshua an inflatable snow tube.

"Do we just count to three and go for it?" Isabel asks.

"Hold on. Instead of just racing, can we make a plan?" Acadia says.

"What do you mean?" Joshua asks.

Isabel smiles. "I know that look in your eye, Acadia. Are you thinking about science class yesterday?"

"Yep," answers Acadia. "Yesterday we learned about energy and friction. To give the sled more speed, it helps to have less friction. That beautiful, fresh, powdery snow is going to create a lot of friction."

"Is friction like drag?" Joshua asks. "Drag was what slowed down our paper airplanes, right?"

Isabel replies, "Yes. You want your sled to have as much energy as possible. Friction takes speed away from the sled. Less speed means the sled won't go as far. More speed means more fun."

Acadia notices some footprints leading toward a nearby spot on the hilltop. She follows the footprints until they stop, and all that remains is the track of a sled heading downhill. "I have my strategy. I'm going to follow these sled tracks. Whoever sledded earlier has packed down the snow here, and the compacted snow will make less friction. Less friction means more speed, and like Isabel said, more speed means more fun."

"How about if we each get to have our own strategy?" Joshua asks. "I'm going to give my sled a running start."

"Good idea. That will give your sled more kinetic energy to start with," Isabel explains.

"What's that?" Joshua asks.

"Anything in motion has kinetic energy," Isabel answers. "We like kinetic energy. Sleds stop when they run out of kinetic energy."

"So my sled will have extra energy from my running, but because I'm in the fluffy snow, I'll also have more friction. It's a tradeoff. But I'm a superfast runner, so I'm not worried," Joshua says in a joking voice while giving Acadia an intimidating look.

Acadia smiles at Joshua and shakes her head. "Not gonna happen."

"Hey, don't count *me* out," Isabel says, as she walks along the top of the hill. "My strategy is that I'm going to find the steepest part of the hill to go down." Isabel finds her spot and sits on her sled.

"Sounds like we all have a plan. Everyone ready?" Acadia asks. The other two nod, indicating yes. "Let's see whose strategy is best. Ready, set, go!"

Joshua steps a few feet back, then runs holding his snow tube. He jumps face-first onto the tube, landing with a bounce. The snow tube starts off fast, but a large plume of powdery snow comes up in his face. His speed quickly decreases as the tube plows down the hill, flattening the snow as it journeys downward.

Isabel's plastic sled also travels quickly at first but is slowed down by the fluffy snow. Her sled displaces the snow by squishing it down and pushing it out toward the sides.

Unlike the other sleds, which push snow out of their way, Acadia's sled squishes the snow down on the already established tracks as it travels. Acadia sits crisscross on her saucer sled and glides so fast that her hair blows back. She clings to the saucer's handles and can't help but shriek with excitement as she gains speed. Her sled goes beyond the tracks and slows down in powdery snow just a few feet farther than Joshua and at least twenty feet past Isabel.

Acadia jumps up. "I won!"

Isabel runs toward Acadia. "Awesome ride! Friction really does make a difference."

Joshua adds, "Each time we go, it'll get even better because the snow will be more packed down. I bet if I do a running start onto Acadia's track, I'll go superfast."

"Let's see what happens if we do a running start onto my track on the steepest part of the hill," Isabel suggests. "Then we can see how our strategies work when they're all combined."

"Sounds good to me," Acadia says as she grabs her sled.

"Let's race up the hill!" Joshua yells, looking back at Acadia and Isabel.

"Why is everything a race with him?" Acadia asks Isabel as they both start to run.

The three huff and puff and smile on their journey back up the hill, enjoying every moment of this beautiful winter day.

Later in the day, Acadia sees a big cardboard box in her family's recycling bin and comes up with an experiment to test friction. She tests the speed of a marble on four different surfaces: cardboard, felt, sandpaper, and glitter.

My Friction Experiment

My question: What track surface will cause a marble to travel the slowest?

Research: I learned that friction impacts the acceleration and force of an object by creating resistance.

Hypothesis: If a marble travels down four different track surfaces (cardboard, felt, glitter, and sandpaper), then it will travel the slowest down the sandpaper because it feels the roughest against my hand, so I think it causes the most friction.

Procedure:

1. Find a large cardboard box and create equal lanes with different materials.
2. Angle the cardboard so there is a starting hill.
3. Make sure the person lets go of the marble at the same height each time.
4. Have one person hold the stopwatch and say "3, 2, 1, go."
5. On "go", one person lets go of the marble and the other person starts the stopwatch.
6. Once the marble hits the bottom stop the stopwatch.
7. Repeat three times for each lane (this helps the results be more accurate).

8. Repeat the process for the next track(s) until all data is collected.

9. Find the average for the trials for each track.

Materials: Marble, cardboard, marker, felt, glue, glitter, sandpaper, stopwatch

Data from My Friction Experiment

Surface	Trial 1	Trial 2	Trial 3	Average (add up the three trials and divide by 3)
Cardboard	0.85 seconds	0.96 seconds	0.78 seconds	0.86 seconds
Felt	1.15 seconds	1.21 seconds	1.16 seconds	1.17 seconds
Glitter	1.06 seconds	1.19 seconds	1.15 seconds	1.13 seconds
Sandpaper	1.02 seconds	1.02 seconds	1.07 seconds	1.04 seconds

Conclusion: The measurements were hard to make because the marble rolled so fast. It was important to do more than one trial because the results were not always consistent, and it was hard to be accurate with the stopwatch. If I did this again, I would make the track longer and maybe try something that doesn't roll, like a cube.

I did find that the cardboard was the fastest track, but the other three tracks were so similar that it is hard to know for sure how they ranked. Therefore, my results are inconclusive.

NEW SCIENCE WORDS

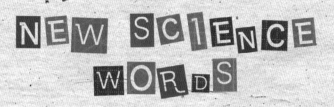

Acceleration

A change (increase or decrease) in the velocity of an object. This change is the combined result of all the forces acting on the object.

Small force = small acceleration

Same force, half the weight = double the acceleration

Same force, double the weight = half acceleration

Force

The amount of a push or a pull. A force changes the motion of an object (that is, it accelerates the object's motion!) unless it's opposed by another, equal force. A force might start a stationary object moving; it might slow or stop an object in motion (like the brakes of a train); or it might change an object's direction of motion without affecting its speed. You apply force to bicycle pedals to turn them and move your bicycle forward, unless the hill becomes so steep that gravity prevents you from going any farther.

NEW SCIENCE WORDS

friction

The resistance that occurs when two objects rub against each other. Friction increases with the area and the roughness of the surfaces in contact. Friction also increases with the force that presses the two objects together. A heavy car develops more friction on a road surface than a light car. For an object moving through a fluid (like an airplane through air!), the friction is called drag. Friction converts kinetic energy into heat, which is why you can start a fire by rubbing two sticks together. Sometimes we want friction, and sometimes we don't. A flying airplane minimizes friction with its aerodynamic design so it doesn't have to burn as much fuel to overcome the drag, but that same plane needs friction between its tires and the runway when it's taking off or landing.

Static Friction

Force → No motion ← Friction

Sliding Friction

Force → Sliding Motion ← Friction

Rolling Friction

Force → Rolling Motion ← Friction

NEW SCIENCE WORDS

Kinetic Energy

The energy an object has when it is in motion.

Potential Energy

The stored energy that an object has because of its position or condition. A stretched rubber band has potential energy. A coiled spring has potential energy. A boulder on top of a high hill has potential energy. Potential energy can be converted into kinetic energy.

Things I Still Wonder:

- Does friction act the same on land, air, and water?
- If there were no friction, would a kicked soccer ball keep rolling forever?
- If my sled runs into a wall (or a person!) and stops short, is that because of friction? When does resistance stop being friction and become a collision? (p.s.: Sorry for running into you, Dad!)

- My dad says that velocity is speed in a certain direction. He says if I ski down a hill in a zigzag path, my speed across the snow is greater than my velocity down the hill. I need to think about this!

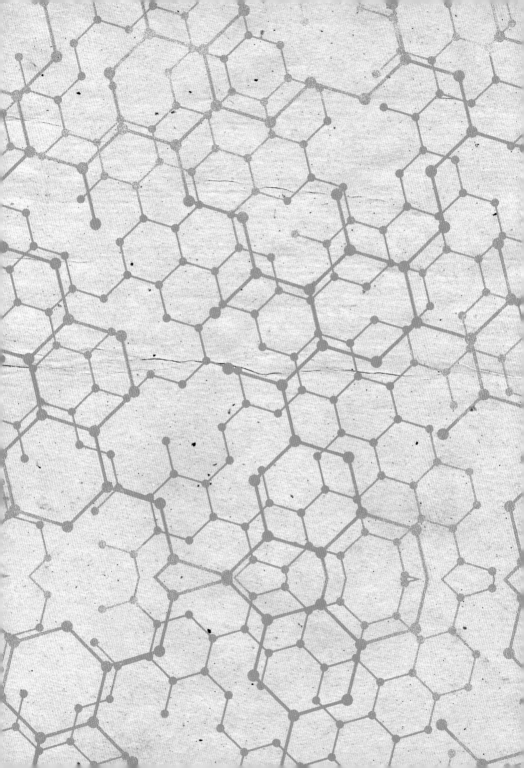

Further Exploration

The following websites were helpful to me while writing this book and are likely to remain active and helpful to teachers and learners in the years to come.

Climate Change (Chapter 1)

https://climatekids.nasa.gov/climate-change-meaning/

https://timeforchange.org/what-is-a-carbon-footprint-definition

https://water.usgs.gov/edu/activity-watercontent.html

http://css.umich.edu/factsheets/carbon-footprint-factsheet

Cutting down on Food Waste (Chapter 1)

http://www.actionforhealthykids.org/game-on/find-challenges/cafeteria-challenges/1510-reduce-food-waste

https://www.fns.usda.gov/school-meals/creative-solutions-ending-school-food-waste

Recycling and Repurposing Items (Chapter 1)

https://kids.niehs.nih.gov/topics/reduce/index.htm

https://www.recyclart.org/

https://artprojectsforkids.org/category/view-by-theme/recycle/

http://kidshealth.org/en/kids/go-green.html

Periodic Table of Elements (Chapter 2)

https://www.eia.gov/KIDS/energy.cfm?page=periodic_table

Atoms/Molecules (Chapter 2)

https://www.orau.org/center-for-science-education/files/build-an-atom/index.html

http://americanhistory.si.edu/molecule/02mol.htm

Neutral Buoyancy (Chapter 2)

http://pbskids.org/scigirls/games/aqua-bot-html5

Paper Airplanes (Chapter 3)

https://www.grc.nasa.gov/www/k-12/airplane/glidpaper.html

http://www.pbs.org/parents/adventures-in-learning/2013/12/straw-paper-airplanes-diy/

http://www.exploratorium.edu/exploring/paper/airplanes.html

https://www.scientificamerican.com/article/bring-science-home-paper-planes-drag/

Aerodynamics (Chapter 3)

https://www.nasa.gov/audience/forstudents/k-4/stories/nasa-knows/what-is-aerodynamics-k4.html

http://www.kids.ct.gov/kids/cwp/view.asp?q=330926

Winter Animal Survival (Chapter 4)

https://www.sciencenews.org/blog/wild-things/eight-ways-animals-survive-winter

https://mainelakesresourcecenter.org/2017/01/30/cold-blooded-winter-survival-of-our-amphibians-and-reptiles/

Animal Tracks (Chapter 4)

http://www.maine.gov/sos/kids/about/tracks.htm

https://www.maineaudubon.org/news/winter-wildlife-tracks/

Physics of Sledding (Chapter 5)

http://iditarod.com/edu/friction-sleds-and-why-its-important-to-get-it-right/

http://msue.anr.msu.edu/news/teaching_science_through_sledding

Acknowledgments

A huge thank you to Jonathan Eaton and the staff at Tilbury House Publishers for believing in this project. Thank you to Holly Hatam for capturing Acadia's journal with her beautiful illustrations.

My husband, Andrew, can be seen throughout these stories by those who know him. He gave feedback and ideas from the first draft through the final revisions. Thank you for the support you show me and the support you always give our family.

Thank you to my grown-up beta readers Andrew McCullough, Lindsay Coppens, and Peggy Becksvoort. Each of you brought a unique lens that made the book better. Thank you to my kid beta readers Greta Holmes, Sylvia Holmes, Isabel Carr, Allison Smart, and Greta Niemann for your honest (and very fun to read!) feedback. And thank you to my students at Falmouth Middle School; the sorts of questions you ask were with me as I wrote the stories and created a vision for Acadia's notebook.

And last but certainly not least, thank you to my fact checkers who helped edit and review the accuracy of the scientific content: Andrew McCullough, Grant Tremblay, Elise Tremblay, Sarah Dawson, Eli Wilson, Jean Barbour, and Bernd Heinrich, who generously answered a question no one else could. A lot of minds and a lot of knowledge are behind this book. I couldn't have done it without them.

Brendan Bullock

KATIE COPPENS lives in Maine with her husband and two children. She is an award-winning middle school language arts and science teacher. Much inspiration from this book came from her marriage to a high school biology teacher and from their focus on raising children instilled with compassion, curiosity, and creativity. Katie's publications include a teacher's guide for the National Science Teachers Association, *Creative Writing in Science: Activities That Inspire.* She welcomes you to visit her at *www.katiecoppens.com.*

Children's book illustrator and graphic designer HOLLY HATAM (Whitby, Ontario) loves to combine line drawings, photography, and texture to create illustrations that pack energy and personality. Her picture books include *What Matters* (SONWA children's awards honorable mention), *Dear Girl, Tree Song* and the picture book series *Maxine the Maker.*

Other ACADIA FILES Books

BOOK ONE
SUMMER SCIENCE

BOOK TWO
AUTUMN SCIENCE

"An excellent series that will help its audience look at the world in a new way."
— Foreword Reviews

"Citizen science that is accessible for young readers."
— Youth Services Book Review

Tilbury House Publishers
12 Starr Street
Thomaston, Maine 04861
www.tilburyhouse.com

Hardcover ISBN 978-0-884448-607-7
eBook ISBN 978-0-88448-609-1

First hardcover printing September 2019

15 16 17 18 19 20 XXX 10 9 8 7 6 5 4 3 2 1

Library of Congress Control Number: 2019941097

Cover and interior designed by Holly Hatam and Frame25 Productions
Printed in the United States of America

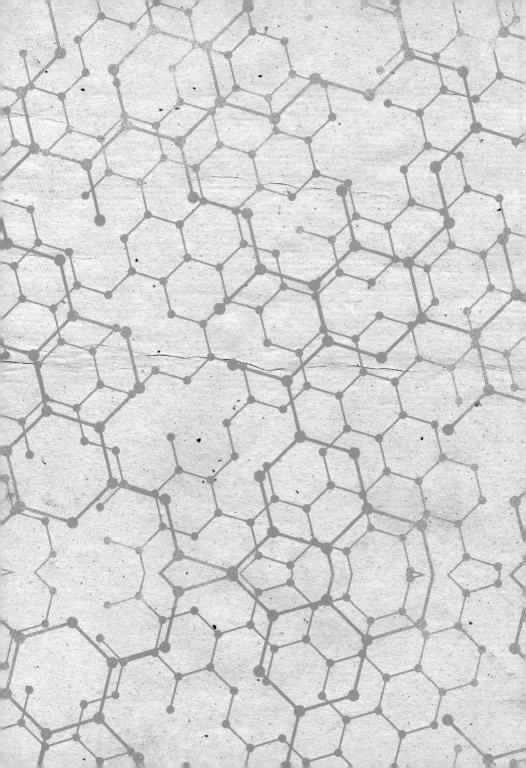

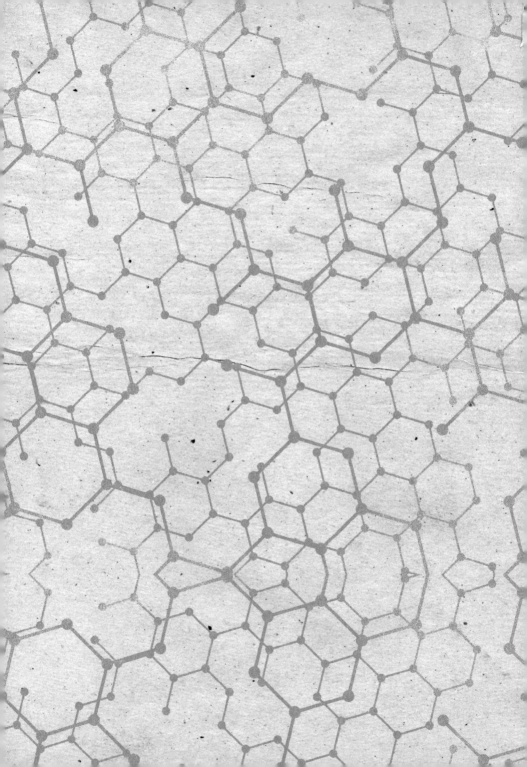